SMART FELLER FELLER FART SMELLER

AND OTHER SPOONERISMS

BY JON AGEE

MICHAEL DI CAPUA BOOKS

HYPERION BOOKS

1844-1930

THE REVEREND DR. WILLIAM ARCHIBALD SPOONER, a beloved professor at Oxford University, England, was not only intelligent and witty, he was also an albino, somewhat shy, and notorious for flip-flopping the initial sounds of words. To the student who wasted a whole term, he said, "Son, you have tasted a whole worm." Toasting the Queen's birthday, he blurted out: "Let's hear it for our queer old dean!" Presiding at a wedding, he told the groom, "It's kisstomary to cuss the bride." There was no explanation for Spooner's embarrassing habit, other than the simple fact that his mouth couldn't keep up with his brain.

Of course, we all make these verbal mix-ups from time to time. And thanks to the good reverend, we have a name for them.

WHAT DID IT SAY
ON THE FRAGILE PACKAGE?

WHAT DID THE BAKER SAY
ABOUT PINOCCHIO'S TALL TALE?

WHAT DID MRS. BONE SAY
TO HER VERY HELPFUL SON?

WHAT DID THE YOKEL SAY
TO THE CUTE LITTLE GIRL?

WHAT DID THE NEW EMPLOYEE SAY
ABOUT HIS TINY CUBICLE?

WHAT DID RAPUNZEL SAY
TO THE FILTHY GIANT?

WHAT DID THE KID DECIDE TO DO
WHEN HALLOWEEN WAS OVER?

WHAT DID THE CYCLIST NEED
TO WIN THE TOUR DE FRANCE?

WHAT DID THE OLD LADY SAY
TO THE RUDE CHILD?

WHAT DID THE BUTLER SAY
TO THE GUY WHO WALKED IN FROM THE SWAMP?

WHAT DID THE ANNOUNCER SAY
TO BEGIN THE RACE?

WHAT DID THE THEATER CRITIC SAY
ABOUT THE REALLY BAD PLAY?

WHAT DID THE TRUCKER ORDER
FOR LUNCH?

WHAT DID GRANDPA SAY
TO HIS FAVORITE GRANDDAUGHTER?

WHAT DID THE TOURIST SAY
ABOUT THE NILE?

WHAT DID THE FRUIT LOVER GET
IN THE MAIL?

WHAT DID THE STOCKBROKER SAY
ABOUT THE ECONOMY?

WHAT DID THE BASKETBALL PLAYER SAY
WHEN HE SLAMMED INTO THE DOORWAY?

WHAT DID THE CLASS GENIUS DO
AT SCHOOL?

WHAT DID THE PICKY EATER SAY
ABOUT DINNER?

WHAT DID THE WEATHERMAN SAY
ABOUT THE SOGGY FORECAST?

WHAT DID THE HOST SAY
AT THE NEW YEAR'S EVE PARTY?

WHAT DID THE MOVIE USHER SAY
TO THE GUY WHO GOT THERE LATE?

WHAT DID THE COWBOY SAY
TO THE ROCKET SCIENTIST?

WHAT DID THE LAWYER SAY
IN DEFENSE OF HER CLIENT FRED?

WHAT DID THE RABBIT FANATIC SAY
WHEN HE SMACKED HIS ELBOW?

WHAT DID THE PROFESSOR SAY
TO THE STUDENT WHO WAS LATE FOR CLASS?

WHAT DID THE GARDENER SAY
TO HER ASSISTANT?

WHAT THEY SAID	WHAT THEY MEANT TO SAY
CANDLE WITH HAIR	HANDLE WITH CARE
THAT'S A LACK OF PIES!	THAT'S A PACK OF LIES!
THANK YOU FOR CHEWING THE DOORS	THANK YOU FOR DOING THE CHORES
YOU HAVE SUCH A DIRTY PIMPLE	YOU HAVE SUCH A PURTY DIMPLE
WHAT A NOSY LITTLE COOK!	WHAT A COZY LITTLE NOOK!
YOU NEED TO SHAKE A TOWER	YOU NEED TO TAKE A SHOWER
TRAMPLE THE SEATS!	SAMPLE THE TREATS!
A WELL-BOILED ICICLE!	A WELL-OILED BICYCLE!
YOU HAVE VERY MAD BANNERS!	YOU HAVE VERY BAD MANNERS!
PLEASE SHAKE OFF YOUR TWOS	PLEASE TAKE OFF YOUR SHOES
GENTLEMEN, CART YOUR STARS!	GENTLEMEN, START YOUR CARS!
THAT WAS A DROWSY LLAMA!	THAT WAS A LOUSY DRAMA!
I'LL HAVE THE CHILLED GREASE SANDWICH	I'LL HAVE THE GRILLED CHEESE SANDWICH
LET ME GIVE YOU A HAIR BUG!	LET ME GIVE YOU A BEAR HUG!
THIS LIVER IS WRONG!	THIS RIVER IS LONG!
A PLATE OF CRUMBS?	A CRATE OF PLUMS?
BAD NEWS CAN MAKE YOUR SOCKS STINK	BAD NEWS CAN MAKE YOUR STOCKS SINK
I HANGED MY BED!	I BANGED MY HEAD!
HE BURNED A LUNCH	HE LEARNED A BUNCH
I REFUSE TO EAT PARROTS AND KEYS!	I REFUSE TO EAT CARROTS AND PEAS!
EXPECT MORE ROARING PAIN!	EXPECT MORE POURING RAIN!
ANOTHER DEER IS YAWNING	ANOTHER YEAR IS DAWNING
I'LL SEW YOU TO A SHEET!	I'LL SHOW YOU TO A SEAT!
YOU SURE ARE A FART SMELLER!	YOU SURE ARE A SMART FELLER!
BREAD IS NOT A FRUIT	FRED IS NOT A BRUTE
OW! I HIT MY BUNNY PHONE!	OW! I HIT MY FUNNY BONE!
YOU HISSED MY MYSTERY LECTURE!	YOU MISSED MY HISTORY LECTURE!
PLEASE PUT THESE PANTS IN THEIR PLOTS	PLEASE PUT THESE PLANTS IN THEIR POTS